For Teresa, my Halloween date!

G. P. Putnam's Sons

An imprint of Penguin Random House LLC, New York

G. P. Putnam's Sons is a registered trademark of Penguin Random House LLC.

Visit us online at penguinrandomhouse.com

Library of Congress Cataloging-in-Publication Data
Names: Rex, Michael, author.
Title: We're going on a goon hunt / Michael Rex.
Other titles: We are going on a goon hunt
Description: New York: G. P. Putnam's Sons, [2020] | Summary: A family treks through spooky landscapes looking for a monster, only to run back home when they actually find one.
Identifiers: LCCN 2019029708 (print) | LCCN 2019029709 (ebook) | ISBN 9781984813626 (hardcover) | ISBN 9781984813640 (kindle edition) | ISBN 9781984813633 (ebook)
Subjects: CYAC: Monsters—Fiction.
Classification: LCC PZ7.R32875 Wc 2020 (print) | LCC PZ7.R32875 (ebook) | DDC [E]—dc23
LC record available at https://lccn.loc.gov/2019029708
LC ebook record available at https://lccn.loc.gov/2019029709
Manufactured in China by RR Donnelley Asia Printing Solutions Ltd.
ISBN 9781984813626

10   9   8   7   6   5   4   3   2   1

Design by Semadar Megged and Suki Boynton
Text set in Martin Gothic
The artist used pencil drawings colored in Photoshop
to create the illustrations for this book.

We're going on a goon hunt.
We're gonna catch a green one.
What a spooky night!
We're not scared.

Uh-oh! A pumpkin patch!

A twisted, tangled pumpkin patch.

We can't go over it.

We can't go under it.

Oh no!

We have to go through it.

Stumble grab,

stumble grab,

stumble grab!

We're going on a goon hunt.
We're gonna catch a green one.
What a spooky night!
We're not really scared.

Uh-oh! A swamp!
A murky, bubbling swamp.
We can't go over it.
We can't go under it.

Oh no!
We have to go through it.

Gurgle hiss, gurgle hiss,

gurgle hiss!

We're going on a goon hunt.

We're gonna catch a green one.

What a spooky night!

We're just a little scared.

Uh-oh! A tunnel!
A dingy, dusty tunnel.
We can't go over it.
We can't go under it.

Oh no!
We have to go through it.

Flutter skulk,

flutter skulk,

flutter skulk!

We're going on a goon hunt.
We're gonna catch a green one.
What a spooky night.
We're a little more scared.

Uh-oh! A forest!
A shadowy, knotted forest.
We can't go over it.
We can't go under it.

Oh no!
We have to go through it.

Grumble stomp,

grumble stomp,

grumble stomp!

We're going on a goon hunt.
We're gonna catch a green one.
What a spooky night!
Now we're really scared!

Uh-oh! A graveyard!

A foggy, crumbling graveyard.

We can't go over it.

We can't go under it.

Oh no!

We have to go through it.

Whisper groan, whisper groan,

whisper groan!

We're going on a goon hunt.
We're gonna catch a green one.
What a spooky night.
Now we're really, *really* scared!

Uh-oh! A haunted house!

A creaky, crooked haunted house.

We can't go over it.

We can't go under it.

Oh no!

We have to go through it.

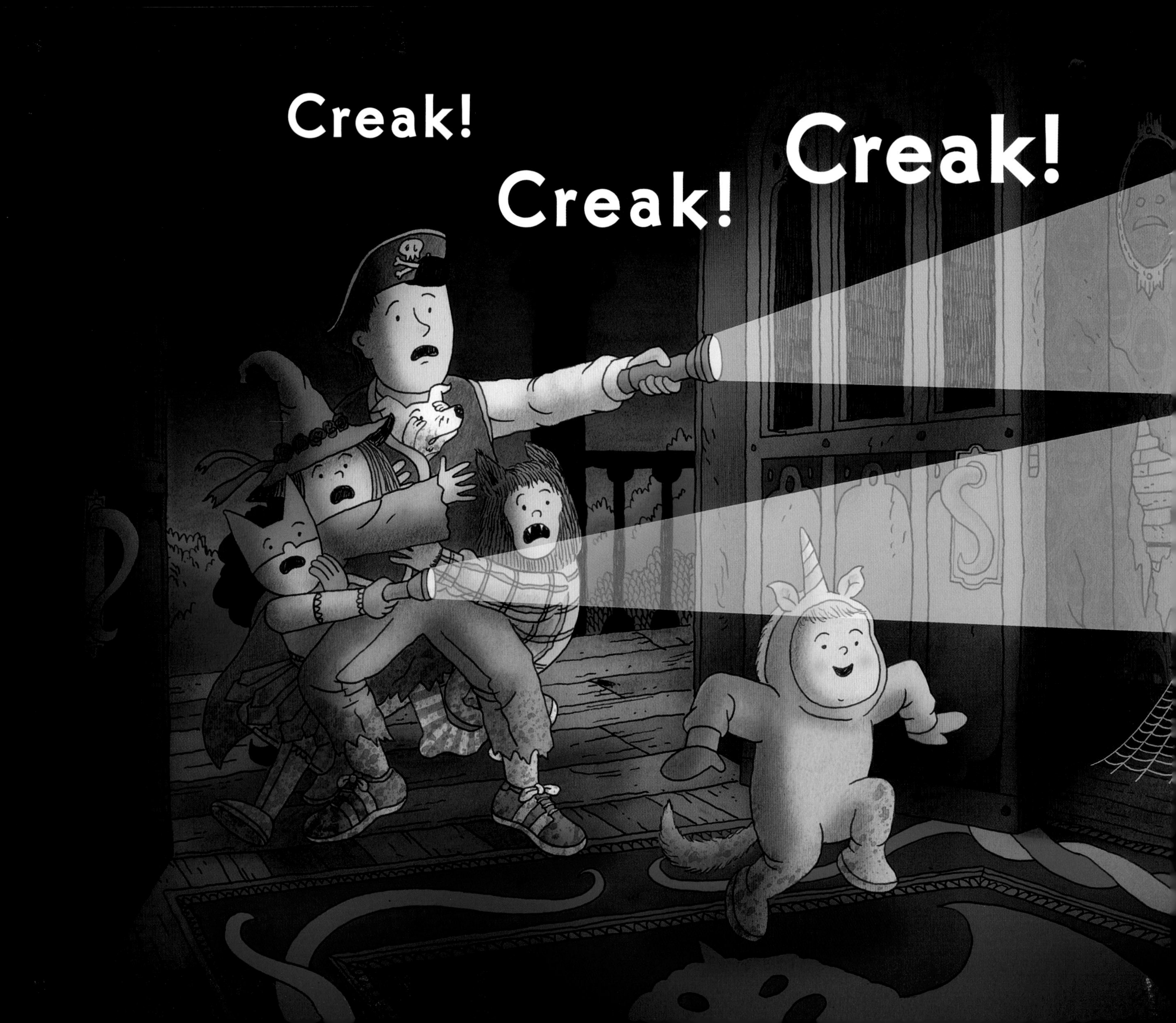

Creak!

Creak!

Creak!

What's that?

One bumpy bald head!

Two big green ears!

Two little beady eyes!

It's a goon!

Quick! Back
through the
haunted house!
Creak, creak!

Back through
the graveyard!
Whisper groan,
whisper groan!

Back through
the forest!
Grumble stomp,
grumble stomp!

Back through
the tunnel!
Flutter skulk,
Flutter skulk!

Back through
the swamp!
Gurgle hiss,
gurgle hiss!

Back through
the pumpkin patch!
Stumble grab,
stumble grab!

Get to the front door!
Open the door.
Up the stairs.

Oh no!
We forgot to shut the door.
Don't go back!

Keep running!
Into the bedroom.
Into bed.
Under the covers.

We're not going on
a goon hunt again!